THE PUPPY PLACE

COOPER

THE PUPPY PLACE

**Don't miss any of these
other stories by Ellen Miles!**

THE PUPPY PLACE

COOPER

ELLEN MILES

SCHOLASTIC INC.

ISBN 978-0-545-60382-9

Cover art by Tim O'Brien
Original cover design by Steve Scott

12 11 10 9 8 7 6 5 4   14 15 16 17 18 19/0

Printed in the U.S.A.   40

First printing, March 2014

CHAPTER ONE

"Are we ready, then?"

Charles rummaged through his backpack, trying to find the navy blue folder. He was sure he had put it in there, but where was it?

"Mr. Peterson?" The booming voice thundered even more loudly. "Are we ready?"

Ah! There it was. Charles pulled out the folder.

"Hello? Charles Peterson? I'm talking to you."

Charles felt his cheeks growing hot, a sure sign that he was blushing. Knowing that his cheeks were bright pink made him feel even more self-conscious, which only made his cheeks pinker. "Yes, Mr. Green . . . I mean, okay . . . I mean, I'm here. And I have my script." He waved the folder in the air, and a bunch of papers fell out of it. They fluttered to the floor, creating a snowdrift around his feet. "Oh." He squatted down to scoop up the papers, juggling the folder as he tried to grab as many sheets as he could. The girl standing next to him bent to help.

The man at the front of the room — Mr. Green — sighed loudly and rolled his eyes. "Okay, people," he said. "This is exactly the kind of thing I was talking about. We're actors, but we're really more like a sports team. To do well, we have to depend on one another, and everybody has to do their best. This play is going to be wonderful — but only if every single one of us works hard. We don't have much time left before opening night, so we need to come prepared and ready to work together. And by now, we shouldn't need our scripts anymore. We should all have our parts memorized. Does everyone understand?" He folded his arms, waiting.

Charles closed his eyes. How had he gotten himself into this? He hadn't, that's how. His mom had gotten him into it. "I signed you up for something really special," she'd told him one day after school a few weeks earlier. "Remember that time I interviewed Mary Thompson about a play she was writing, about the history of Littleton?"

"I guess," said Charles. His mom was a reporter for the local paper, the *Littleton News*. She had interviewed just about everybody in town, including Mary Thompson, who was a famous writer. (She was the author of one of Charles's favorite picture books ever, *So Many Puppies*.)

"Well, she finished the play, and now the Littleton Players are going to put it on," Mom said. "It'll be part of the big birthday celebration for our town. There are some parts for kids in it, so I signed you up for auditions. I thought you'd like to try out for a role."

Charles stared at his mom. "You did? Why?" An actor was about the last thing Charles wanted to be. "I don't even like to give oral reports at school," he reminded her.

Mom nodded. "Exactly. Being in a play will give you so much self-confidence. You know, I was shy, too, when I was your age. Then my best friend convinced me to be in the Christmas pageant one year. We were both angels, and we had such fun. Somehow, after that, I was much less shy." She smiled encouragingly at Charles.

"I'm not that shy," Charles said. "It's just that there are a lot of other things I'd rather do." He looked down at the puppy by his side. "Like play with Buddy."

Buddy glanced up at Charles and thumped his

tail, the way he always did when he heard the word "play." His ears perked up hopefully.

Buddy was the best friend Charles had ever had. He was a little brown-and-white puppy with a huge personality. Buddy had come to stay with the Petersons as a foster puppy (Charles's family took care of puppies who needed homes). Most of the puppies were only with them for a short time, but Buddy had never left. Everybody had fallen in love with him: Mom, Dad, Lizzie (Charles's older sister), Charles, and the Bean (their younger brother) all adored Buddy. He was part of the Peterson family now.

"You'll still have plenty of time with Buddy," said Mom.

By the way she said it, Charles knew her mind was made up. He was trying out for that play whether he liked it or not.

The next Saturday, Mom drove Charles to the town hall, a big brick building that housed the town offices, a theater, and meeting rooms. "You'll have fun, honey," she said as they walked up the stairs to the theater, where the auditions were being held.

She was wrong. Charles did not have fun at all. For one thing, nobody had told him that the play was a musical, which meant that as part of his tryout, he would have to sing. By himself. In front of everybody.

When he found out, Charles closed his eyes and wished with all his might for the auditions to be over. It didn't work. He watched as dozens of grown-ups and kids belted out songs they had prepared. Some were good singers, some not so great, but one by one they all got up there on the small stage at the front of the room and did their stuff. They smiled at Mr. Green, the director, and at Mrs. Davies, the music director. Charles could tell that most of these people really, really wanted to be in the play. Some of them even added little dance steps to their routines.

When it was Charles's turn, he could not think of a single song to sing. He stood onstage, his cheeks getting hotter by the second. Finally, he opened his mouth.

"The worms crawl in, the worms crawl out," he sang. *"The worms play pinochle on your snout."*

Somebody giggled. Somebody else snorted. A moment later, everybody in the room was laughing. At Charles.

Even Mr. Green laughed, a booming laugh that was as big as his voice. "Fantastic!" he bellowed. He called the very next day to tell Charles he'd gotten a part in the play. "You'll be playing Jasper, the youngest son in one of the families," he said. "You're perfect for the role. And Mrs. Davies thought your singing was charming. She can't wait to work with you."

Now, at rehearsal, Mr. Green still stood waiting with his arms folded. "Does everybody understand?" he asked again.

Charles tucked the last piece of paper into his folder. "Yes!" he shouted along with everyone else. But he didn't. After two weeks of rehearsals, he still didn't understand how this could be happening to him. Why couldn't he memorize his lines or learn the songs they had to sing? He felt self-conscious whenever he was onstage, and he didn't know what to do with his hands. Mr. Green wasn't mean, but he had very high expectations, and that made Charles nervous. At least Mrs. Davies was nice. She was always smiling and laughing and telling stories about when she used to be on Broadway. Where was she, anyway? Charles looked at the piano that sat just below the stage, off to one side. The piano bench, Mrs. Davies's usual perch, was empty. He noticed Mr. Green checking his watch and looking at the door. He must be wondering, too.

A few minutes later, as Mr. Green was reviewing the rehearsal schedule, Mrs. Davies flew through the door, breathing hard. "Sorry I'm late," she said. "It's this one's fault." She pointed down at the floor by her feet. Charles craned his neck. What he saw immediately made him feel a whole lot better.

It was a puppy.

CHAPTER TWO

It was a very funny-looking brown-and-white puppy. It had big bat ears, a long nose, a long, wide sausage-shaped body, a feathery tail, and the shortest legs Charles had ever seen on a dog. The pup trotted along happily at Mrs. Davies's feet, keeping up with her as she strode to the piano. Charles couldn't help smiling as he watched. Mr. Green smiled, too, but he shook his head. "A dog, Evelyn?" he asked. "Really?"

"I'm sorry," Mrs. Davies said again. "This is Cooper. I had to bring him. He's only a baby, six months old. If I leave him at home alone he gets bored and starts destroying things." She sat down at the piano bench. "Sit, Cooper," she said. "Good boy." She opened a book of music and set it on the piano, then turned to Mr. Green. "I promise he'll behave."

Charles looked at the girl next to him. Maribel played his character's sister, Grace. She and Charles were in all the same scenes together, and they'd gotten to be friends. "How can she even tell if he sat or not?" he whispered. "His legs are so short."

Maribel giggled. "He's cute, though."

"Really cute," Charles agreed. He was dying to pet Cooper. "I think he might be a corgi." Charles did not know as much about dog breeds as his sister Lizzie did, but he remembered seeing a picture of a corgi once and noticing the big ears.

"Ahem." Mr. Green cleared his throat.

Charles looked up to find Mr. Green looking at him. Oops. "Sorry," he said. Right. He was supposed to be paying attention to the director, not the puppy.

"All right, people," said Mr. Green. "We'll start from the beginning of the play. Act one, scene one. Cast members not in this scene, please take a seat."

Almost everyone left the stage, including Charles and Maribel. The only people in the first act were Ed Williams and John Stark, who played the original settlers of Littleton.

Like every kid in Littleton, Charles had heard the story of his town's founding many times. Before the town was a town, Ebenezer Wetmore and Jebediah Smythe had carved out homesteads on opposite sides of Turkey Hill. For the first few months, neither of them knew that the other was there. Then, one day when Ebenezer was cutting trees for firewood, Jebediah turned up and started yelling at him. "This is my land, you fool!" he said.

"Your land? This is my land!" Ebenezer yelled back.

The men argued, and the famous family feud began. From then on, it was the Wetmores against the Smythes.

Now the actors playing the original settlers stood onstage while Mr. Green explained the way he wanted the scene to go. "You'll enter from the left," he told Ed Williams. "And when you see Ebenezer, you'll be surprised, then angry. You'll stop right about here" — he pointed to a spot on the stage — "and start shouting."

Mr. Green had explained that what they were doing now in rehearsals was called "blocking," when the director told the actors where they should be onstage and the play began to come to life. As far as Charles was concerned, blocking was boring. It took forever to get through each scene. It was hard, too. He was learning a lot of theater terms, like "stage right" (which confusingly meant the audience's left) and "wings" (the area just offstage where actors waited to make an entrance). It was like a whole new language.

He worked his way over to the piano. So far, he had been a little shy around Mrs. Davies, but he couldn't stay away from that puppy for a minute longer.

"Cute puppy," he whispered. "Can I pet him?"

Mrs. Davies nodded, and Charles sat down on the floor and let the puppy come to him. "Hi, Cooper," he said very softly when the puppy sniffed at his hand. Cooper seemed like a happy, confident pup. He greeted Charles like an old friend, climbing right up into his lap. Charles giggled when the dog licked his face. Cooper's tail thumped against Charles's leg.

Hey, pal!

"He likes you," whispered Mrs. Davies.

"I like him, too." Charles stroked the dog's soft, thick fur as Cooper settled down with a contented sigh. The puppy's wide body was surprisingly heavy, but he was small enough to mostly fit on Charles's lap. For the first time since play rehearsals had started, Charles felt at home.

Mrs. Davies looked down at the puppy and shook her head. "Such a cutie," she said in a low voice. "He's the fourth corgi I've helped to rescue, and I thought I was going to be able to keep this one. But now I'm not so sure."

Charles knew about groups that "rescued" certain breeds. His family had once fostered Scout, a puppy who had come to them through a German shepherd rescue: people who loved the breed and stepped in to help out whenever they heard about a dog who needed to find a new home. "Why can't you keep him?" he asked.

Mrs. Davies glanced up at Mr. Green to see if he was ready for her to play some music, but he was busy explaining how he wanted Ebenezer to hold his ax.

"I just got a lead role in a big musical at the Dunston Playhouse," Mrs. Davies told Charles. "It's great, but I have to drive an hour each way to get there for rehearsals. Between this job and that one, I'm hardly ever home. It's not fair to Cooper."

Charles looked down at the funny pup in his lap and felt his heart skip a beat. "Maybe I could help," he whispered back. "My family fosters puppies."

"Evelyn?" Mr. Green called from the stage. "We're ready for you."

Mrs. Davies sat up straight, riffled through the pages of music on her stand, and struck the opening chords of the play's first song: "This Is My Land." Then she turned toward Charles and, still playing, winked at him and whispered, "We'll talk later."

CHAPTER THREE

Charles sat with Cooper on his lap, watching the two men onstage sing a silly duet in which each tried to top the other, over and over again. Their deep voices rang through the room as they belted out the song. Mrs. Davies pounded chords on the piano, sneaking a smile and a wink at Charles every so often.

Charles petted Cooper's soft ears. "How do they do it?" he asked the pup. He knew the men were actors, but they seemed so natural and so confident. He could not imagine ever feeling that comfortable onstage.

With a final flourish of notes, Mrs. Davies brought the song to an end. The men struck their final poses, then stomped off to opposite sides of the stage. "Perfect!" shouted Mr. Green. "Fabulous!" The men popped out of the wings, grinning. They took silly bows as the rest of the cast applauded.

"That's the kind of energy I want to see up here," said Mr. Green. "Don't save it for performances, people. Bring it here, a hundred percent, every single day." He looked down at the papers in his hand. "Okay, let's go on to scene two. Smythe family parlor. Actors onstage."

Charles hugged Cooper. "I have to put you down," he whispered into the thick ruff of fur around the puppy's neck. Cooper squirmed around so that he could lick Charles's cheek.

Can't I come with you?

Charles gave the puppy one last hug and set him on the floor, handing his leash to Mrs. Davies.

"He'll be fine," said Mrs. Davies. "And so will you." She gave him a broad smile and one last wink.

Charles climbed the stairs to the stage, leaving his backpack — with the script in it — on his chair. After all, he had only three lines in this scene. He should be able to remember them.

Mr. Green moved busily among the actors, placing people where he wanted them. He sat Charles and Maribel on a bench at stage right. "When we have our full set, this will be a couch," he told them. "But for now you'll just have to pretend."

By now, Charles knew that "set" meant all the things — furniture, pretend walls, scenery — that made a play look like it was happening in a real place.

"Okay." Mr. Green stepped back down into the audience. "Let's run through the scene."

Maribel had the first line. She turned to Charles. "I've never seen Papa so angry before," she said. "What do you suppose is the matter?"

Charles opened his mouth, but no words came out. He twisted his hands together and closed his eyes tight, as if that would help him remember his line. The room was so quiet that Charles could hear Mr. Green's frustrated sigh. Finally, it came to him. "I don't know," he said, with his eyes still closed. "But it has something to do with a man named Ebenezer Scrooge."

"Argh!"

Charles opened his eyes and saw Mr. Green staring at him, hands on hips. "Ebenezer Scrooge?" the director asked. "I think you've got your stories mixed up." His lips twitched, and suddenly he was smiling. "Kind of funny, really." He chuckled, then let out a booming laugh. Everybody in the room joined in.

Charles wasn't sure whether they were laughing at him or with him. In fact, he wasn't even sure what the joke was until Maribel whispered to him. "Ebenezer Scrooge is a character in that story *A Christmas Carol*," she said. "You know, the one with the Ghost of Christmas Past and Tiny Tim and all that?"

Charles felt his face getting hot again. They were laughing *at* him. The character in this story was Ebenezer Wetmore. He knew that. He'd just forgotten.

"Okay, people," said Mr. Green. The laughter finally died down. "Let's move on with the scene. We'll back up and take those lines again."

This time, Charles got his line right. But he flubbed the line after that, and when Mr. Green told him to stand up and move to stage left for his next line, he moved to stage right by mistake. Why couldn't he stop messing up?

"Let's take five, people." Mr. Green sounded tired.

That was one theater phrase Charles had learned early on. It meant that it was time for a five-minute break, which you could use to go to the bathroom, or go outside and get a breath of fresh air, or look over your script again, or whatever. Charles knew what he wanted to use his five minutes for: Cooper. He headed straight for the piano. "Want me to take him out for a minute?" Charles asked. "Maybe he has to pee."

"Sure," said Mrs. Davies. "I'll come with you."

Outside, they watched as Cooper trundled along on his short little legs, checking out the bushes that towered over him. Even the grass came up to his knees! Charles felt his mood lift. "He's so cute," he said to Mrs. Davies. "And he's really mellow. Not too many puppies would just settle down that way."

"He's smart, too," she said. "The woman who originally rescued him told me that he already knows ten tricks. I really hate to have to give him up, but it's just not fair to a puppy to leave him home all the time."

"My aunt Amanda runs a doggy day care," Charles told her. "Maybe you could take him there."

"I wish," said Mrs. Davies. "The trouble is I can't afford it. I'd be spending all the money I'm earning just on dog-sitting."

"Let me talk to my mom when she comes to pick me up," said Charles. "If she meets Cooper, maybe she'll say we can foster him. We would take really good care of him. We've fostered a lot of puppies, so we have a ton of experience."

"Wow," said Mrs. Davies. "That would be —"

24

"Break's over," called one of the other actors from the doorway.

Charles was hoping that Mr. Green would choose to move on to another scene, one that he was not in, but instead the director called the same actors up onstage. "We need to get this scene polished," he said. "Let's give it one more try."

Charles groaned. He bent down to give Cooper a good-bye pat.

Mrs. Davies went over to Mr. Green and whispered something into his ear. The director raised his eyebrows. Then he looked at Charles and Cooper. "Really?" he asked Mrs. Davies. "You think it would work?"

She nodded.

"I suppose it's worth a try," said Mr. Green. "Charles, bring the dog up onstage with you."

CHAPTER FOUR

"Bring the dog?" Charles asked. He wasn't sure he had heard right.

Mr. Green nodded. "You can keep him on your lap while we run through the scene. Mrs. Davies seems to think he'll help you feel more comfortable onstage."

Charles grinned down at Cooper. "Let's go, pal!" He led the dog up the stairs to the stage. Cooper trotted along happily on his stubby little legs.

Yes! I was hoping we could go up here. I like the look of this.

As they crossed to their spot on the bench, Cooper seemed even happier. He held his head and tail up and walked with a special bounce. Charles heard Mr. Green laugh. "Look at him," said the director. "What a little ham."

Charles took his seat next to Maribel. "Ham?" he whispered. "Does he mean that Cooper looks like a pig?"

She giggled. "He means that Cooper likes being onstage. That's what they call someone who loves to be dramatic: a ham."

Charles nodded. "I'm no ham," he said. "Most of the time I'd rather be doing just about anything else." He pulled Cooper onto his lap and petted the puppy's soft fur.

Mr. Green clapped his hands. "Everyone ready?" he asked. "Let's take it from the top of scene two."

Just as she had earlier, Maribel turned to Charles. "I've never seen Papa so angry before," she said. "What do you suppose is the matter?"

"I don't know," said Charles. "But it has something to do with a man named Ebenezer Wetmore."

The words spilled out easily this time. Charles and Maribel went on with their dialogue, and — for the very first time onstage — Charles said every one of his lines perfectly. He could tell how surprised Maribel was, and when he snuck a glance at Mr. Green, he saw that the director was grinning.

Charles felt more comfortable onstage than he ever had before. The warm weight of Cooper on his lap, and the way the puppy gazed up at him as he spoke, made everything seem normal. He felt almost like he was in his own living room, talking to Lizzie, with Buddy on his lap.

"Magnificent!" Mr. Green applauded loudly,

and the rest of the cast joined in. "And now, let's run through the song."

This song, "It Used to Be So Peaceful," started as a duet between Charles and Maribel, and then other Smythe family members joined in.

Mrs. Davies thumped out a few chords on the piano. "Ready?" she called out. "And . . ."

"It used to be so peaceful, up here on Turkey Hill," sang Charles. His voice was stronger than usual, and he hit the high note just the way Mrs. Davies had taught him.

"But storm clouds are brewing," Maribel sang back, reaching out to pet Cooper. *"I know you feel it, too."*

Right in time, Cooper sat up on Charles's lap and let out a mournful howl.

Charles wanted to laugh along with everyone in the audience, but he did his best to stay in character and stick with the song. *"It's a darker day now, up here on Turkey Hill,"* he sang, squashing down his giggles.

"But if we stick together, we Smythes will see it through," Maribel sang back.

Cooper howled again, right along with the music.

This time, everybody laughed, even the other cast members onstage. Mrs. Davies was laughing so hard she couldn't play anymore, and the piano went silent.

Cooper hopped off Charles's lap, shook himself, and stretched out his front legs with his behind up in the air, as if he were taking a bow.

Thank you, thank you. I'm so glad you can all tell what a star I am.

The laughter grew even louder, and everyone applauded and cheered.

"Well," said Mr. Green as the laughter died down. "I'm not sure we want to make this song into such a comedy, but I have to say that Cooper seems very comfortable onstage. Maybe he was named after Gary Cooper, the famous movie star."

Mrs. Davies laughed. "Maybe he was. He came to me with that name, and it does seem to fit him."

"In any case, thank you, Cooper," said Mr. Green. "I think we'll work on that song some more tomorrow. For now, let's move on to scene three."

Charles was relieved to be able to leave the stage and let the next group of actors take over. It was great that he had done well, but he'd had enough for now. He headed down the steps with Cooper.

"Charles!"

He peered into the darkness of the room. "Mom?"

"Hi, honey." Mom gave Charles a hug. "That

was amazing. I finished up my errands so I got here early to pick you up. Mr. Green always says it's fine for parents to watch." She leaned over to pet Cooper. "And this little guy was really something else. I never saw a dog steal the show like that before."

Charles smiled down at Cooper. "So, you like him?" he asked his mom.

"He's completely adorable," she said.

"Guess what?" Charles asked.

CHAPTER FIVE

It was easy to convince Mom to foster Cooper; Charles could tell that she was already half in love with the pup just from watching him onstage. After they talked to Mrs. Davies about it some more, they called home. Dad was fine with the idea, too. "A corgi?" he asked when Charles told him about Cooper. "Aren't they those long, low footstool-type dogs?"

"Dad!" Charles said. "Cooper is no footstool." In the background, he could hear Lizzie asking excited questions.

"A corgi? We're fostering a corgi? Is it a Pembroke

or a Cardigan? Girl or boy? Does it have a tail? When do we get it?"

Charles heard Dad laugh. "Easy, Miss Lizzie," Dad said. Then he spoke into the phone again. "Sure, bring the little guy home. Is he okay around kids? I'm about to go pick the Bean up from day care."

"He's fine," Charles reported.

The Petersons always made sure that any foster puppies they took in would be safe around a toddler like the Bean.

Mrs. Davies had already told Charles and Mom that Cooper loved little kids. "Other dogs, too," she'd said. "The rescue group gave him a complete evaluation, and he came out with flying colors. He gets along with everybody."

Now, on the phone, Dad chuckled. "Guess I'll pick up some extra puppy food while I'm out, too. Looks like we've got a guest coming to stay."

Charles could hear Lizzie's whooping even when he held the phone away from his ear. He felt like whooping, too — but rehearsal was still going on, so he just grinned at Mom as he handed back her phone.

The rest of rehearsal went by in a flash. Charles brought Cooper onstage with him whenever he was in a scene, and the same magic seemed to work each time. Charles got his lines right and remembered all the words to the songs. He even got a "well done!" from Mr. Green for helping Mrs. Schneidwind (the lady who played his mother) with a line she'd forgotten.

Cooper, meanwhile, kept getting laughs and applause for the funny things he did, like rolling over onto his back and waving his short legs in the air, or jumping up to lick Charles's chin right when Charles was in the middle of a serious speech.

"I hate to see him go," said Mrs. Davies when rehearsal was over. "But I know it's the right thing." She checked her watch. "I have to drive home, grab something to eat, and drive to Dunston for another rehearsal. Oh, and I have to practice one of my songs as I drive, since I didn't have any time earlier today. I wouldn't have a moment to spare for Cooper." She bent to kiss his nose. "I know you're in good hands," she told him. "You be a good boy."

Cooper was a good boy. He rode politely in Mom's van, and when they got home, he climbed out and walked happily and confidently up to the door.

As long as I'm with nice people, I'm sure everything will be fine.

Lizzie flung open the front door. "Cooper!" she cried. "Oh, he's a Pembroke Welsh — and a total cutie." She ran out and kneeled down to say hi, and Buddy bolted out the door behind her.

"Hey," Mom said. "I thought we had a rule about how Buddy meets our foster pups. Aren't we supposed to give them each some space, out in the backyard?"

"Oops," said Lizzie. "I guess I was too excited to remember about that. Sorry. But look! They're getting along great."

Buddy sniffed Cooper. Cooper sniffed Buddy. Their tails wagged.

"I'm so glad he has his tail," said Lizzie. "Some Pembrokes are born without them. But if a puppy is born with a tail, breeders usually dock it. I don't think that's very nice."

"What does 'dock' mean?" Charles asked.

"It means they cut it off," said Lizzie. "They do it when the puppy is really tiny, and supposedly it doesn't hurt — much. But still."

"Why do they do it?" Charles liked Cooper's tail. He would never have cut it off.

Lizzie shrugged. "It's just the way those dogs are supposed to look."

Cooper wasn't interested in their conversation. His tail wagged some more and he put out his paws toward Buddy in a play bow.

Friends?

Friends!

From that moment on, nobody could separate the two puppies. Out in the backyard, they ran and played. Buddy leapt right over Cooper. Cooper rolled over onto his back with his bat ears straight out and paddled his feet at Buddy. They chased after balls and drank out of the birdbath, and finally, they collapsed in a furry heap together, exhausted from all the fun.

When Dad and the Bean got home, Cooper ran to greet the new people. The Bean stood still and held out his hand, as he'd learned to do with dogs he didn't know. Cooper sniffed gently, then wagged his tail and gave the Bean's hand a soft lick. The Bean laughed his googly laugh, and Dad laughed along as he bent down to pet the new puppy. It was official: all the Petersons were in love with Cooper.

That night, Charles practiced all his lines from the play, over and over. He wanted to show Mr. Green that he really had memorized the script. Cooper was a big help. Charles pretended that the puppy was the other actor in each scene, and he looked into Cooper's soft brown eyes as he said his lines. Cooper couldn't answer, but that didn't matter.

Charles recited his lines to Cooper as the puppy followed him around while he set the table, and he said them again as he helped dry the dishes with Cooper sitting at his feet. He performed them in the living room in front of his family, holding Cooper on his lap.

He said his lines while he got ready for bed — with Cooper watching as he brushed his teeth — and he muttered them as Dad tucked him in, with Cooper lying at the foot of his bed. He even dreamed some of his lines as he slept, while Cooper snored softly.

When it was time to leave for rehearsal the next day, Charles felt ready — really, really ready. He was going to show Mr. Green — and everybody else — that he could say his lines, and sing the songs, without bumbling or messing up once.

All he needed was a little puppy magic. With Cooper by his side, Charles felt completely confident. "Let's go, Cooper," he said, snapping a leash onto the puppy's collar.

"Uh-uh," said his mom. "Cooper is staying home."

CHAPTER SIX

"What? Why? What do you mean?" Charles stared at his mom. He must have heard her wrong. Why would he leave Cooper at home? Cooper had to come to rehearsal.

Mom put a hand on Charles's shoulder. "Cooper and Buddy are getting along so well," she said. "Don't you think he'd rather be here, playing with his new friend?"

"But he liked being at rehearsal," Charles said. "He's a ham. He loves making everybody laugh."

"Be that as it may," said Mom, "Cooper is staying here. Mr. Green doesn't want a dog at rehearsal. It's much too distracting. It's one reason we're fostering Cooper in the first place, isn't it? So that Mrs. Davies doesn't have to bring him every time?"

Charles knelt down and threw his arms around Cooper's thick neck. He rubbed his face on the puppy's soft fur and whispered into his big bat ears. "You want to come, don't you?"

Cooper wagged his tail and panted into Charles's face.

You bet I do!

"Charles, it's time to go," said Mom.

Charles stood up. He was about to start begging for Cooper to come, but one look at Mom's face told him that there was no point. Her decision was final. Cooper was staying home.

* * *

"All cast members onstage," called Mr. Green, clapping his hands. "We're going to start with some singing today. I want to polish up all our songs. Then we'll run through the whole show. Don't forget, people — this is production week. Dress rehearsal tomorrow, performances on Friday and Saturday. It's almost showtime."

Charles groaned to himself, but everyone else looked happy and excited.

Mr. Green waved toward the piano. "Mrs. Davies, can you warm us up?"

Charles trudged up the short staircase to the stage, behind Maribel. He usually loved their singing warm-up, but today he just couldn't get excited about it. His stomach was fluttery and his mouth was dry. He wished he were holding the script that was stuffed in his backpack, which was sitting on a seat in the auditorium. How was he going to remember a single line, or a single note of a song, without Cooper there?

Mrs. Davies stood up by her piano. "Ready, everyone?" she asked when they were all onstage. Then she let loose two long, high notes: "Sooooo-weee!"

Charles usually cracked up along with everyone else when she did that, but today he didn't even smile. "Sooo-weee!" was a hog call, something Mrs. Davies had learned to do when she was a girl on a farm. She'd used it as a singing warm-up ever since.

"Soooo-weeee!" everyone sang back.

Mrs. Davies reached down to the piano and struck a note. "Soooo-weee!" she called, one note higher than before.

"Sooo-weee!" they all sang back, on the same note.

Up and down the scale they went, until Mrs. Davies nodded and sat down to strike the first chord of the song "Stay Away from Those People," from the second act. She played the introduction, then glanced up at the actors onstage, cuing them to come in.

"Soo-wee!" yodeled Charles while everyone else sang the first line of the song.

Mrs. Davies stopped playing. Everybody turned to look at Charles.

"What?" he asked. "Oh. Whoops. Sorry!" Charles realized that he hadn't been paying attention. He'd been too busy wondering what Cooper and Buddy were doing, and wishing Cooper were right there by his side, "singing" along with him.

Mr. Green frowned. "Let's take it from the top," he said. "Is everybody ready?" He gave Charles a meaningful look. "Everybody?"

Charles knew his face was red. He nodded. "I'm ready," he whispered. This time, when Mrs. Davies played the first notes of the song, Charles sang along — or at least, he pretended to. He moved his mouth, but no sound came out. He knew he wouldn't do the "soo-wee" call again, but he was afraid he'd get the notes wrong. He didn't want Mrs. Davies to have to start the whole song over.

After they had sung most of the songs in the show, Mr. Green called for a run-through of act one, scene four. Charles groaned as most of the actors headed off the stage, leaving him and Maribel alone.

"Now remember, this is an important scene," Mr. Green said. "This is where the real story starts. Let's make sure the audience hears all the details and understands what's going on."

Maribel nodded. Charles nodded, too, looking down at his hands, clenched together in his lap. His empty lap. Where was Cooper when he needed him? If he could just pet that soft fur and feel the puppy's weight on his legs, everything would be fine.

Maribel patted Charles's arm. "You'll be okay," she whispered. Then she turned to the audience and said, in a loud, clear voice, "You'll never believe what I saw today, up by the waterfall."

"What did you see?" Charles asked. He knew his voice sounded stiff and weird, but he couldn't help it. At least he had gotten his line right.

"I saw Joseph and Faith kissing!" Maribel said.

Those were the names of the oldest boy in the Smythe family and the oldest girl in the Wetmore family. Their secret romance was about to become public — and help change the course of history by bringing the families together.

"Our brother? And Faith Dembowski?" As soon as his line came out, Charles knew it was wrong. Dembowski was the last name of the actress who played Faith. Charles moaned and put his face in his hands. Then he looked up again, in time to see Mr. Green shaking his head. "I mean, Faith Wetmore," Charles finished lamely. "I'm sorry, Mr. Green."

He saw Mrs. Davies get up to whisper in Mr. Green's ear. Mr. Green nodded. "Take five," he said tiredly. He waved at Charles. "Come talk to me." He patted the seat next to his.

A few minutes later, Charles was on the phone to his mom. "Mom?" he asked. "Can you bring Cooper down here?"

CHAPTER SEVEN

"We're raising the roof, raising the roof! A home for our family, raising the roof!"

Charles sang along, grinning as he hit the high notes. Everything felt right, now that Cooper was back onstage with him. He looked down at the little dog. As usual, Cooper seemed completely comfortable. He smiled his own doggy smile and howled along happily. His bat ears twitched as he gazed up at Charles.

Isn't this fun?

The roof-raising song was in the first scene of the second act. The stage was full of people: all the men and boys in the Smythe family, plus some distant cousins and other settlers who had come to help.

In the play, the Smythes were moving up in the world, building a real house to live in instead of their tiny, rough cabin. After this song, the spotlight would shift to a scene between two boys: Joseph Smythe and a boy named Patrick, who was a bit of a stranger. The twist here was that Patrick was not a boy. It was Faith Wetmore, dressed up to look like a boy so she and Joseph could see each other even though their fathers had forbidden them to meet. The audience would understand when they saw her hair spilling out from beneath her cap as she and Joseph kissed behind the barn.

"Raising the roof, raising the roof!" Charles sang

the last notes of the song as loudly as he could, smiling down at Mrs. Davies. She winked at him as she pounded out the final chords on the piano.

In the audience, Mr. Green clapped loudly. "Fantastic!" he said. "Exactly what I'm looking for. I love the energy, and you're all hitting your notes perfectly. Terrific. Now, let's move on to Joseph and Faith's duet. Everybody else offstage for now."

Mrs. Davies played the introduction to the next song as Charles and most of the other actors headed down into the audience. Jillian Dembowski pulled off her cap and let her hair tumble out. *"A love like ours,"* she sang, *"can't be hidden forever. A love like ours must bloom someday."*

She had a sweet, high voice, but Charles did not really like this song. It was too goopy and embarrassing, all that love stuff. He gestured to Maribel as he headed to the back of the auditorium. "Let's play with Cooper," he whispered.

As they walked up the aisle, he saw someone sitting alone in the very last row. "Charles!" the person called. When he was close enough, he saw that it was Mary Thompson.

"Hi," he said. "What are you doing here?"

"Taking some notes," she said. "Mr. Green called me a little while ago and asked me to come down. He wants me to do a little rewriting on the play." She reached out to pet Cooper. "He was right about this pup. What a cutie."

"He told you about Cooper?" Charles knew that Mary Thompson was a dog lover.

"He sure did," said Mary. "In fact —"

"In fact, she's going to write Cooper into the play," said Mr. Green, slinging himself into a seat next to the author.

Charles stared at him. "Cooper's going to be in the play?" he asked.

Mr. Green smiled. "Look, Charles. I actually have

complete faith that you could do your part perfectly with or without that puppy on your lap. But at this point I don't know if I have time to convince *you* of that. So yes, in the play Jasper and Grace Smythe will now have their very own puppy. I think the pooch will add a lot to the show."

Charles felt his belly roll over at this reminder that time was running out. Showtime, that weekend! Yikes. But then he reached down a hand to pet Cooper's thick fur, and he smiled. So what? He could do it. He would have his pal at his side.

Mary Thompson cleared her throat. "You know," she said to Mr. Green, "a corgi is not exactly historically accurate. I think the settlers would have been more likely to have some kind of mutts, or maybe spaniels."

Mr. Green waved a hand. "I know, I know," he said. "But have you seen what this little guy can do? The audience is going to love him."

Mary Thompson smiled at Cooper and reached down to scratch him between the ears. "It's true, he's very lovable."

Charles wondered whether Mary might be interested in adopting Cooper, but maybe now was not the time to ask. "He's smart, too," he said. "He knows ten tricks already."

"Does he?" asked Mary. "What are they?"

"We're not sure," said Charles. "So far we've only figured out nine." He counted on his fingers as he listed them. "He can sit and shake, and lie down and roll over, and play dead —"

Cooper sat, then held up a paw, then plopped all the way down on the floor with his chin between his paws. Everybody cracked up, and he looked up at them with a "what's the big deal?" expression. Then he rolled over as quick as a wink, jumped to his feet, and flopped back down on his side and lay very still, playing dead.

Just following orders!

"Those are great," said Mary. "I'm sure I can work some tricks into the scenes. For example, maybe you could tell him to sit when your father comes into the room in act two." She scribbled some notes on the script she had on her lap.

Charles nodded. "He can also S-T-A-Y and C-O-M-E," he spelled out so Cooper wouldn't get confused. "And S-I-T P-R-E-T-T-Y."

Mary Thompson looked puzzled. "What was that last one? Sit pretty?"

Immediately, Cooper sat up on his back legs with his front paws held out.

Everybody laughed again.

"A star is born," said Mr. Green.

CHAPTER EIGHT

"This shirt is so itchy," Charles whispered to Maribel. They stood together in the wings, waiting for their cue to go onstage. It was dress rehearsal night, and everything was different. Instead of a T-shirt, Charles was wearing a rough brown blouse that he'd pulled on over his head. Instead of jeans, he wore knickers, also made out of some scratchy kind of cloth. He was barefoot, and he wore a tan cap. And lipstick.

"What? No way!" Charles had said when the makeup lady came at him in the dressing room. But she didn't listen. She put stuff on his cheeks that made him look like he was blushing times one hundred, darkened his eyebrows with a brown pencil, and dabbed red color onto his lips.

"Everybody has to wear makeup, girls and boys," the woman said calmly as she puffed powder all over his face with a wide brush. "Otherwise the stage lights will make you look like a ghost. Trust me, dearie, from the audience you'll just look normal. Nobody will be able to tell you have stuff on your face."

Charles didn't believe her, but there was no getting out of it. She was right; all the actors and actresses had makeup on. Maribel's lips were even redder than his.

For dress rehearsal, they were running straight through the whole play. The first scene was already under way. Charles's heart beat hard as he looked out at the stage. It had been totally transformed. The two actors playing Jebediah

Smythe and Ebenezer Wetmore stood arguing in front of a painted forest. Ebenezer swung his ax, pretend-chopping a pretend tree — flat, painted wood propped up in back so it wouldn't fall over.

Bright lights beat down on the stage. Charles tried to peek at the audience, but he could only make out dark forms filling some of the seats. He knew Mom was out there, and Mary Thompson — and a bunch of other people, mostly friends and family of cast members. This was their largest audience so far, and on performance nights there would be even more seats filled.

Charles reached down to pet Cooper. Having the puppy with him made all the difference. Yes, he was nervous — but he knew he could do it, as long as he had his friend by his side. Cooper looked up at him and wagged his tail.

Almost our turn, pal!

The actors onstage finished their dialogue, and Mrs. Davies began to play the chords that introduced their song. *"This here, this is my land,"* sang Jebediah.

Charles took one deep breath, and then another, the way Mr. Green had taught them. He knew what was going to happen next. As soon as the song was over, the stage would go dark. Stagehands would scurry out to take away the tree and replace it with indoor furniture: a table, chairs, the couch where Charles and Maribel would sit. The painted forest would rise on ropes, and the pretend walls of a living room would come down. The actors would take their places. The stage lights would go on again, and Maribel would speak her first line. Then it would be Charles's turn.

He took another deep breath.

And then, it all began to happen, just the way it was supposed to. Charles found himself sitting on the red couch (more scratchy material) next to Maribel. He pulled Cooper onto his lap. The stage lights blazed on, warming Charles's face. He gulped, petted Cooper, and gulped again. Maribel was talking. And then it was time to answer her, saying his first line. He pulled Cooper closer.

"I don't know," he said. "But it has something to do with a man named Ebenezer Wetmore." It came out perfectly, and the knot in Charles's belly loosened.

After that, time seemed to speed up. The whole play went by like a movie on fast-forward. Cooper performed perfectly whenever Charles gave him his cues to sit or lie down, and he got a big laugh when he rolled over at the end of the "Raising the

Roof" song. Before Charles knew it, he was back onstage with the entire cast, taking a final bow as the audience applauded like mad. Mr. Green, in the wings, grinned and gave them all two thumbs up. "Fantastic dress rehearsal, everyone," he called. "Absolutely fantastic!"

The cast filed off the stage, and most of the actors went right into the audience to talk to friends and family members who had come to watch. Charles took Cooper up the aisle. They both needed a moment outdoors.

"Charles," Mom called, and waved. "You were wonderful!" She ran to hug him.

Of course, she had to say that. She was his mom. But then Mary Thompson waved him over. "Terrific job, Charles," she said.

The man next to her nodded and smiled. "Well done." He stuck out his hand. "I'm Mary's friend Ted Maxley," he said.

Mom gave Charles a little touch on his back. "Introduce yourself," she said.

But before Charles could say his name, Cooper took a few steps closer to the man, sat, and offered Mr. Maxley his paw.

Mr. Maxley's eyebrows went up. Then he grinned and bent low to shake the puppy's paw. "Very nice to meet you," he said to Cooper. "You did a terrific job, too."

Cooper's ears twitched and his tail thumped the floor.

Thanks. It's great to have fans.

Charles and his mom looked at each other and laughed. "I guess Cooper knows how to introduce himself. That must be trick number ten," said Mom. She explained to Mr. Maxley how they'd discovered each of Cooper's tricks.

"Yes, Mary told me that this fellow was quite an entertainer," said Mr. Maxley. "I came here with her tonight so I could meet him. I understand you're fostering him?"

"That's right," said Mom.

"I think I may know of a wonderful home for Cooper." Mr. Maxley turned to look straight at Charles. "There's only one thing. I'd have to take him to meet someone — tomorrow."

"But tomorrow is the play's opening night," Charles said. Of course it was important to find a good home for Cooper, but what about the play? Charles knew he couldn't manage without the puppy onstage with him.

"I understand. I promise to have him back in time for the show," said Mr. Maxley.

"You can trust Ted," said Mary. "He's one of my oldest friends, and he's very good with dogs. Cooper will be safe with him."

Charles knew he had no choice. The whole point of fostering puppies was to find them good homes. He had to let Mary's friend take Cooper. Everything would be okay, as long as the puppy really was back in time.

CHAPTER NINE

Cooper was not back in time.

Cooper was not back when Charles was working hard to swallow the cheese sandwich Mom made him eat before he went to the theater. He was not back when they got into the van to drive to the town hall. No puppy appeared while Charles was putting on his costume, or having his makeup done, or listening to Mr. Green's opening-night pep talk. Everyone in the cast was beyond excited, because they'd heard that an agent, a person who helped actors get parts in plays and movies and TV, was in the audience that night. Charles didn't care about that at all, since he never wanted to be onstage again — ever.

Now Charles stood in the wings, just as he had the night before during dress rehearsal. He watched the two actors pretend-fight in front of the pretend forest. Everything was just the same — except that Cooper was not at his side. No twitching ears, no thumping tail, no bright eyes looking back into Charles's.

Charles groaned. He felt Maribel touch his arm. "It's going to be all right," she whispered. "You'll be fine."

That was exactly what Mr. Green had said. "You'll do fine." He had patted Charles on the back. "Remember, I have complete confidence in you — with or without Cooper. You know your lines, you know the songs, you're all set. Just take a few deep breaths right before you go on — and don't forget to skip those new lines Mary wrote about the dog."

By now, Charles had taken so many deep breaths that he felt like he might pass out. How could this have happened? Mary's friend had promised to get Cooper back in time for the show. Charles looked behind him, hoping that Mr. Maxley had shown up at the very last minute. Unfortunately, there was no puppy in sight.

Onstage, the actors were finishing up their song. A moment later, waves of applause, sprinkled with a few whistles and whoops, came from the audience. The stage went dark. The stagehands scurried. And Charles and Maribel stepped onto the stage.

They sat on the couch and waited for the lights to come on. Charles's lap felt so empty without Cooper there to hold. He took one more deep breath and tried to think about what Cooper would do if the puppy were there onstage without Charles. Would Cooper be scared? No way. Cooper would be confident. Cooper would be calm. Cooper would carry on and do his best. All Charles needed to do was try to be like Cooper.

The lights blazed on, and there was a scattering of applause for the new set. Maribel turned to Charles. "I've never seen Papa so angry before," she said. "What do you suppose is the matter?"

Charles concentrated on looking at Maribel instead of the dark mass of people who filled the theater. "I don't know," he answered. "But it has something to do with a man named Ebenezer Wetmore."

Maribel gave him a tiny smile, and they went on with the scene. Charles got every one of his lines right and only flubbed one note in their song. Mrs. Davies winked at him from her piano as she struck the final chords, so he knew she'd heard it. But she smiled, too. When the stage went dark at the end of the scene, Charles sat back and let out a long sigh of relief.

"Keep it moving," whispered a stagehand. "We have to get this couch out of here."

As soon as they were backstage, Maribel pounded Charles on the back. "You did it!"

Charles grinned. "I did, didn't I? I guess it's not so hard after all. But I still miss Cooper."

"I think he missed you, too." Maribel pointed down the hallway. There was Mr. Maxley, leading Cooper toward them. Cooper's ears were up as he trotted eagerly toward Charles.

"So sorry to be late," he said. "Car trouble. Mr. Green said it's fine if Cooper still appears in the play — but not until act two. At intermission Mary's going to give you a line to say about your new puppy."

Charles squatted down to give Cooper a hug. He buried his nose in the thick, soft fur of the puppy's neck. "I'm so glad to see you, pal," he said. Cooper squirmed and thumped his tail and licked Charles's cheek.

Great to be back. I've had some adventures.

"Did you —" Charles wanted to ask Mr. Maxley if the "someone" he'd taken Cooper to meet was interested in adopting a puppy, but the sound of applause told him that the scene had ended.

"We're due onstage!" Maribel said. She grabbed Charles's hand and they ran as fast as they could.

Somehow, knowing that Cooper was in the building made Charles feel even more confident. He got through the entire scene without messing up once and grinned out at the audience when they applauded at the end. He was pretty sure he heard his dad's special whistle, the one he did by putting two fingers into his mouth.

During intermission, Mary Thompson came backstage with Cooper and explained the new line she had written for Charles. "When the next scene begins, you'll say, 'Papa, may I bring the new puppy to the house-raising?'" she said.

"Got it." Charles knelt to scoop Cooper into his arms. Suddenly, he couldn't wait to get back onstage.

CHAPTER TEN

When Charles and Maribel made their entrance after intermission, Cooper pranced right out onto the stage along with them. Charles heard rustling in the audience and some oohs and aahs and exclamations of "He's so cute!" Confidently, he walked up to the man playing his father. "Papa," he said, trying to speak slowly and clearly, "may I bring our new puppy to the house-raising?"

The actor smiled broadly. "Of course! Just keep an eye on him so he doesn't get underfoot."

Once those two new lines were out of the way, Charles relaxed. Everything was going to be all right now that Cooper was there.

Before he knew it, they were into the next scene, the one in which the mothers — who liked the idea of a marriage between their families — planned a picnic where both families would meet. Then there was the picnic scene itself, with Charles's favorite song, "The Picnic Song." Cooper liked that one, too. He always "woo-wooed" along with the happy chorus that went, *"Under the trees we'll eat what we please, a picnic's fine with me!"*

Cooper was even part of the final scene, the wedding that would unite the two families. He sat between Charles and Maribel and barked his approval when the minister, Reverend Little, declared Faith Wetmore and Joseph Smythe man and wife.

At the very end of the scene, Ebenezer Wetmore and Jebediah Smythe began to argue again. Now that their settlement was becoming a real town, they would have to decide on a name — and of course they could not agree. The audience laughed as the two men sang their final song, another version of their first one.

Before Charles knew it, he was holding hands with Maribel as they took a bow together at the front of the stage. This time, he was certain he heard his dad's whistle, along with a "Go, Charles!" from Lizzie. Charles smiled and waved and gave Cooper, who stood in front of him, the sign for "take a bow." Charles and Lizzie had taught Cooper his eleventh trick, and he was good at it. Cooper stretched out his short front legs with his butt high up in the air, the way he did when he wanted to play. The applause and whistles grew even louder.

A few moments later, Charles and Maribel grinned at each other as they waited in the wings. The applause had not stopped, which meant that they had to go out again for a second curtain call. When they walked back onstage, the lights were on and they could see the whole audience standing on their feet, applauding like mad. "A standing ovation," whispered Maribel as she, Charles, and Cooper took another bow. "I guess they liked us."

He saw her scanning the audience. "I wonder where that agent is sitting," she said. "I wonder who he's going to talk to after the show. He could make somebody here into a star."

Charles shrugged. "Who cares? All I know is I can't wait to get out of this scratchy shirt."

When the applause finally ended, all the actors filed offstage. "Well done," said Mr. Green, giving each person a hug as they walked past him. "Fantastic show. Great job."

When Charles and Cooper reached him, Mr. Green whooped. "The stars of the night! You were fantastic." He knelt down to pet Cooper. "The audience was bonkers over this guy."

Cooper stuck close to Charles in the crowded dressing room as Charles changed his clothes and scrubbed the goopy makeup off his face. "Ugh," Charles told the puppy. "You're lucky you don't have to wear lipstick." Cooper thumped his tail and grinned a doggy grin up at Charles.

I'm a natural. Everybody says it.

When Charles and the rest of the cast members stepped into the main theater, a crowd was waiting for them. Parents, brothers and sisters, friends — everybody burst into applause again when they saw the actors. Charles spotted his family near Mrs. Davies's piano and ran to them. "Charles, you were great," said Mom. Dad gave

Charles a high five, and the Bean threw his arms around Charles's legs.

"Cooper was great, too." Lizzie bent down to scratch the puppy's head. "He's really something else. And he and Buddy get along so well. Maybe we should —"

Just then, Charles saw Mary Thompson and Mr. Maxley coming toward them. Mr. Maxley gave him a smile and two thumbs up.

"Was that for the play, or because you found Cooper a home?" Charles asked when Mr. Maxley had made his way through the crowd. Charles was so curious that he forgot to be shy.

"Both," said Mr. Maxley. "The play was fantastic. Mary's writing, your acting and singing — and of course Cooper's role. All great."

"And?" Charles asked.

"And yes, I found Cooper a home." Mr. Maxley beamed down at the short-legged pup. "With me!"

He put a hand into his pocket and pulled out a business card, which he handed to Charles. "I'm an agent," he said. "I specialize in animal actors. I'm also a trainer."

"Wait, you're the agent we heard about?" Charles asked. That was funny.

"That's right," said Mr. Maxley. "My wife and I live on a small farm, with four other dogs, some trained miniature horses, and even some ducks and sheep that Cooper might enjoy herding."

"So . . . who did you introduce Cooper to today?" Charles was confused.

"To a casting director who was looking for a dog for a new movie that is going to be filmed this year. I took Cooper for an audition, and he got the part. Didn't you, Shorty?" Mr. Maxley smiled down at the stubby-legged puppy. "There was no competition. None at all."

Charles glanced at Lizzie, expecting her to look disappointed. She had fallen in love with Cooper, just the way he had. But she was smiling. "Your place sounds like doggy heaven," she said. "And just think — one of our foster puppies is going to be a movie star!"

She and Charles and the Bean all plopped down on the floor and threw their arms around Cooper. "I'll miss you," Charles said into the puppy's soft ear. "But I think you're going to be very happy in your new home."

When he stood up, Charles handed the business card back to Mr. Maxley.

"No, you keep it," said Mr. Maxley. "That way, you can check up on Cooper anytime. Also, please call me if you decide you would like to keep acting. I have an agent friend who works with kids, and I think she'd be very interested in meeting you. You had a real presence up on that stage."

Charles felt himself blushing. He shook his head. "Acting is okay, but there are other things I'd rather do. I think my acting days are probably over after tomorrow night's show," he said. "But I can't wait to see Cooper on the big screen!"

PUPPY TIPS

Some puppies are born to be superstars! I have read more than one article about a rescue dog who ended up with a career in the movies or on TV, and I always thought it would be fun to write about a puppy who could act. It's probably not so easy to break into show business, but you never know. If your dog is cute, clever, and well-behaved, teach her some great tricks. Enter her in a talent show and maybe she'll be discovered, like Cooper was!

Dear Reader,

Wouldn't it be fun to be in a play with your dog? I don't think my hound mix, Zipper, would do very well onstage. He is not so good at sitting still, for one thing. He would rather be chasing squirrels or chewing on something. Still, I like to work on teaching him tricks. (His best one is shaking hands when I say "Introduce yourself!") Maybe someday, when he is a little more mature, we can put on a show for our friends.

Yours from the Puppy Place,
Ellen Miles

P.S. For another story about a dog who likes to perform, check out SWEETIE!

THE PUPPY PLACE

DON'T MISS THE NEXT PUPPY PLACE ADVENTURE!

Here's a peek at STELLA!

"We should be just about there," said Charles's dad. He peered through the windshield of the van. "Watch for a sign that says something about Crystal Lake."

"I see it! I see it!"

Charles turned to stare at his younger brother, the Bean. "What are you talking about?" he asked. "You can't read."

The Bean bounced up and down in his car seat. "Can too, can too!" He pointed out the window. "L is for lake!"

Charles swiveled back around in his seat and stared out his side window, just in time to see a large sign that said, WELCOME TO CRYSTAL LAKE! It had a picture of a lake on it, a bright blue lake surrounded by pine trees.

"He's right!" Dad put on his blinker. "This must be the road we take."

Charles slumped in his seat, feeling tired even though he'd been sitting still for hours. "I still wish Lizzie was with us," he said. "Or that we could have stayed home with her and that new puppy." This camping trip was supposed to have included all the Peterson kids, but at the last minute his older sister had gotten a call from Ms. Dobbins, the lady who ran the animal shelter where Lizzie volunteered. Since the Petersons were known for fostering puppies — taking in young dogs who needed homes — Ms. Dobbins knew just where to turn when she had a puppy she couldn't keep at the shelter. Charles's older sister knew more about dogs than most adults. She had begged Mom to let her stay home and foster the "emergency puppy."

"Mom may not be so happy about the situation, either," Dad said. "She was looking forward to a weekend on her own, when she could really enjoy visiting with her friends."

It was Mom's reunion week, when she got together with three friends from college. One year she had gone all the way to California to see "the girls," but this year they were all coming to Littleton. Mom had been cleaning the house for weeks, and had even bought new curtains for the living room.

"Hey," Dad said. "Forget about Lizzie and the puppy. Let's just have a fantastic boys' weekend, okay? You, me, Buddy, and the Bean. Boys rule!"

Charles had to smile. "Boys rule!" he repeated, looking back at the Bean, happy in his car seat, and at Buddy, curled up peacefully on his soft doggy bed in the wayback.

Buddy was the only foster puppy the Petersons had kept forever. Charles loved him so much, from the tip of his waggy tail to the top of his adorable nose. What could be better than a camping trip with his best pal? Charles sat up straighter in his seat. "How big is this campground, anyway?" he asked.

"I don't know," Dad admitted. "I found it online, and I arranged everything with a few phone calls. The people who run it seem very nice."

"And it has a lake?" Charles asked.

"A lake, and streams, and woods. And I bet

there won't be many people there at all, since the nights are getting cold these days."

"What kind of fish are we going to catch?" Charles asked.

"Well, I don't know. Maybe some bass or a big toothy pike." Dad flashed his teeth at Charles and chomped noisily.

"If I catch a pike, you're taking it off the line," Charles said. He did not like the idea of a big toothy fish.

"Pike!" yelled the Bean. "Pike smike like trike!"

They all cracked up.

"Hey, is this it?" Charles pointed to another sign. "Finster Family Campground?"

"This is it!" Dad said, turning onto the unpaved road. "The man I spoke to said to grab a map from the front porch and go straight on to our campsite."

He pulled the van up to a big brown log cabin with green shutters. "This must be the lodge —

and there's a box with the maps in it," he said. "Hop out and grab one, will you?"

Charles unbuckled and got out of the van. He took a long, deep breath of the fresh, piney-smelling air. It wiped out any sleepiness or grumpiness he had been feeling. He trotted up the broad wooden steps to the wide porch, noticing the green wooden rocking chairs placed all along its length, and pulled a map out of the box labeled CAMPGROUND MAPS. Next to it was a glass case that held a typewritten sheet titled *Finster Family News and Views*. A quick glance told him that it covered campground news, like the weather, the largest fish someone had caught in the last week, and a special feature on bats. There was also a column called "Stella's Story," headed by a blurry picture of what looked like a small white dog. Charles stepped up to take a closer look, but just then Dad beeped the horn. "We'd better keep moving if we want to get ourselves set up before dark," he called.

Charles got back into the van and passed the map to Dad.

Dad passed it back. "You navigate. Our camp-site is the one called Elm. Tell me which way to go."

Charles bent over the hand-drawn map and puzzled out the route to their campsite. "Take a right up there," he said, pointing to a fork in the road just past the lodge. "I think."

Soon they passed the lake — more of a pond, really, but big enough — and wound their way along a twisty road lined with tall pines. "Maple, Oak, Spruce . . ." Charles read the signs in front of each empty campsite they passed. He wondered if they were the *only* campers at the Finster Family Campground. "There it is! Elm!"

ABOUT THE AUTHOR

Ellen Miles loves dogs, which is why she has a great time writing the Puppy Place books. And guess what? She loves cats, too! (In fact, her very first pet was a beautiful tortoiseshell cat named Jenny.) That's why she came up with the Kitty Corner series. Ellen lives in Vermont and loves to be outdoors every day, walking, biking, skiing, or swimming, depending on the season. She also loves to read, cook, explore her beautiful state, play with dogs, and hang out with friends and family.

Visit Ellen at www.ellenmiles.net.